ABOUT LAST NIGHT

O'GALLAGHER NIGHTS
RORY ∞ EMILY

MIGNON MYKEL

Also By Mignon Mykel

LOVE IN ALL PLACES *series*
full series reading order

Interference **(Prescott Family)**
O'Gallagher Nights: The Complete Series
Troublemaker **(Prescott Family)** *
Saving Grace **(Loving Meadows)**
Breakaway **(Prescott Family)** *
Altercation **(Prescott Family)** *
27: Dropping the Gloves **(Enforcers of San Diego)**
32: Refuse to Lose **(Enforcers of San Diego)**
Holding **(Prescott Family)** *
A Holiday for the Books **(Prescott Family)**
25: Angels and Assists **(Enforcers of San Diego)**
From the Beginning **(Prescott Family)**

The Playmaker Duet (Troublemaker, Breakaway, Altercation, Holding)
can be enjoyed in one easy boxed set.

ABOUT LAST NIGHT

O'GALLAGHER NIGHTS

RORY ~ EMILY

MIGNON MYKEL

ISBN: 1539368688
ISBN-13: 978-1539368687

Cover Design and Formatting: oh so Novel
Editor: Jenn Wood
All images and vectors have been purchased.

O'GALLAGHER NIGHTS SERIES

PROLOGUE

The last job I ever saw myself in was working as a barmaid for an extremely popular Irish-American pub. Hey, nothing against waitresses and bartenders. It just wasn't something I ever saw for myself.

At seventeen, I graduated high school a year early only to go straight into nursing school—with many of my gen ed's already completed.

My big plans, the ones that worked so damn well on paper, had me graduating with my Bachelors of Science in Nursing by the age of twenty, with even greater plans of continuing on to eventually become a Certified Nurse Anesthetist. Ideally by twenty five.

I had such great plans.

But just like plans—and life—tend to do, everything sort of fell through the cracks my freshman year of college. My years of overachieving had me burning out by the end of first semester and with failed classes came lost scholarships. I had to drop out of my classes and work double overtime to afford my rent and expenses. I was a nursing assistant at a fairly nice assisted living facility, making bonuses on top of bonuses, and overtime on top of that.

But eventually I burned myself out there too and needed to go back to school.

I was now twenty-four with no degree to my name, but thankfully I was only a semester away from the first one. On paper, my new plan had me graduating the anesthesia program in another three years, so not too far from my original hopes, but I wasn't placing any bets these days.

While I loved my job and the people I worked with, namely

my residents, I needed something that worked better with my schedule and paid extremely well.

Selling myself or finding a sugar daddy were not options.

I was walking down the street and came across O'Gallagher's, an Irish-American pub near both my apartment and school, when I saw a Help Wanted sign in the window. While not something I saw for myself, if I were to work at O'Gallaghers I could get rid of my car—I had nothing against Uber or Lyft—and hopefully make enough in tips working four to eight hours most nights, rather than working twelve hour shifts at the nursing home every night.

I didn't have any sort of experience in the service industry outside of what I did in health care, but I sucked it up and walked into the doors, applying and interviewing on the spot.

Turned out, the O'Gallagher siblings lost a couple of their barmaids with the end of the previous school year and were hoping to expand the business.

Conor, the oldest of the three, was a hunk with his big body and bearded face, tattoos up and down one of his arms, and his sexy ease of wearing a tee and ball cap. Brenna, the youngest, was incredibly sweet and just a bit younger than I.

Then there was Rory.

I'd heard about Rory O'Gallagher. He had a reputation that preceded him.

Rory was the type of guy who made money, flaunted money, and was, frankly, a rude piece of shit.

If you were talking to the girls he dated.

And even dated was too nice of a term.

The girls he fucked.

And left.

He took what he needed from them, gaining respect in their little circles, and then dropped them all like bad habits.

Rory O'Gallagher was not a nice guy.

Sure, he put on a pretty front, but under it all, lay a dirty, rotten, conniving man.

And it would be in my best interest to forever stay clear of him.

CHAPTER ONE

RORY

The first thing I always noticed upon waking was the sun trying to cut through my eyelids.

It was fucking obtrusive. Let a man sleep, yeah? Especially a man who worked until the early morning hours.

Damn sun and its insensitivity.

I know, I know, room darkening shades. But those things cost money, and my money was better spent elsewhere. Well, that and my last apartment had a tiny ass window in the bedroom and didn't warrant the black curtains. The apartment above the bar, where I'd just moved into a few weeks prior, had much better glass to the outside world.

The second thing I noticed was the leg wrapped deliciously around my hip.

Which, of course, led to the third thing, the lovely phenomenon known as 'morning wood.'

Let's be completely open and honest here. I noticed that one every day.

Of the three, it was the leg wrapped around me that gave me slight pause though. I almost always walked my women out at night.

I lifted my eyelids, squinting against the sun, and looked down and over to the body attached to the leg. She was on her stomach, leg up over my hip and face down in the opposite direction. Her contortion didn't look comfortable but then again… I chuckled, remembering the acrobatics of last night.

This chick here swore she'd been an Olympic hopeful in

gymnastics and damn, she had the flexibility to go with that statement, but I highly doubted at twenty-three, Team USA was going to take her. Any other country, sure, but the United States gymnastics team had standards.

And I knew her age because I checked her ID before serving her last night.

Could it have been a fake? I mentally shrugged. Sure, fakes could be damn convincing but as a guy who had a business in college making forgeries, I was going to go ahead and say her license was legit.

She'd been really fucking cute last night, with her halter top and short skirt. This morning though her hair was a bit of a mess. I frowned to myself, taking in the chick's white blonde hair. She was face-down in the bed, the sheet draped low covering her ass, and she was wearing a tank top with those small spaghetti straps. When the fuck did she put clothes on?

I reached down to reposition my dick and frowned when I encountered my boxers. When the fuck did I put clothes on?

I wracked my brain, trying to piece together the night.

I closed the bar last night with Emily. After she left for the night, I talked Cute Halter Top upstairs when all was said and done. She nodded, giggled, and stuck around for me to finish closing up.

We went upstairs, got it on like Donkey Kong...

And then I walked her to her car.

And Em—

I quickly looked down at the girl beside me. Shit.

I leaned over the woman as to not wake her, lifting her hair gently to confirm my fears.

Yep.

Fuck.

Emily.

I sat back and rubbed my palms over my eyes roughly, trying to recall more of the night. We both had clothes on, so it wasn't like I fucked her. That wouldn't go over real well with Conor.

I chuckled. Fuck. That wouldn't go over real well with Emily, either. She fucking hated my guts.

What happened, what happened, what happened...?

I opened the back door for Cute Halter Top, not really paying attention to her as she gabbed on and on. She was a fucking screamer in bed, but she really had to shut her trap now. Too fucking talkative.

I stepped out onto the back step and nearly tripped over something.

"Fuck." Damn homeless people.

But when I looked down, everything jerked to a stop.

"Isn't that your waitress?"

Barmaid was the term we used, but, "Yeah. Here, let's get you to your car." Cute Halter Top and I walked around a sleeping Emily, and I got the girl to her car. I scratched at my chin, trying to figure out what the hell Emily was doing back here, and sleeping on the back stoop no less.

When I reached Emily again, she hadn't moved. In the dim light the back lantern provided, I saw her face streaked with tears and an unfamiliar, unwelcome, clench happened somewhere in the vicinity of my chest.

I knew the girl didn't like me. She wasn't quiet about it. Take tonight, for instance. She didn't normally close with me, but Stone and I switched shifts as a favor to him. When she found out it would be she and I, I almost expected her to walk out.

But I knew her story. I knew why she'd been at O'Gallaghers for the last year. It wasn't because she liked passing out lagers and getting her ass slapped, that was for damn sure.

When she wasn't ignoring me, she was shooting daggers my way and saying some snide comment or another. She wasn't exactly quiet about her distaste of me and my affairs.

I couldn't very well leave her sleeping out here, though. It was September in San Diego; it was starting to get chilly at night, and she was only wearing the tank and shorts she'd changed into after her shift ended.

I bent down and lifted her willowy form. She was tall for a

girl, probably around five-eight, maybe only five-seven, with clear blue eyes and long, white blonde hair that, I swear to fucking God, reached her ass when she let it down and straight. She usually wore it in those big curls girls liked and pulled back in a pony-tail.

She was gorgeous, I wasn't denying it. I just knew she didn't like me so I didn't go out of my way to be overly nice to her.

When I straightened to my full height, she sleepily turned her head into my shoulder, her nose rubbing against my neck, and fucking damn if my dick couldn't seem to remember it was just getting some twenty minutes ago. I was harder than a fucking rock, and all she did was put her nose against my neck. And she didn't even know she was doing it.

Jostling her legs so her knees draped over my forearm comfortably, I made my way back inside, carrying her upstairs. She could sleep in my bed tonight.

But fuck if I was sleeping on the couch.

Playing nice guy fucking sucked. Regardless if she woke up right now, with me staring down at her with a fucking raging hard-on tenting my boxers, or if she woke up after I left to meet with Conor, she would fucking know where she was the moment she found the front door.

I couldn't worry about that now. I had things to do, and Emily could be late for her fucking review with Conor and me. I wasn't about to wake her up and deal with her wrath.

I glanced at the clock. Ten.

Fuck.

I had things to do. As in past tense.

Conor was going to fucking kill me for being late.

Again.

My brother used to be all chill and shit about being late when it dealt with the female variety, even more so when it was him and his dick sunk in some chick's pussy, but then he went and became a dad and now he wasn't so fucking cool any more.

It wasn't like our meeting this morning was all that damn important. We were literally only sitting down and getting ready for yearly reviews.

Woo-fucking-hoo if I was late. I think the only person we were scheduled to sit down with today was the blonde currently in my bed. I couldn't stop the grin at the thought of her in my bed for other reasons. I'd totally do her if she weren't such a bitch to me.

I stretched my arms up above then behind my head, linking my hands and allowing my fist to tap against the wall. When that stretch was in the middle of glory to the heavens, I stretched my legs, pointing my toes, loving the feel of each muscle stretching taut. My movement caused Emily to stir.

When she removed her leg, I crunched up to sit and swung my legs off the bed. I looked over my shoulder as I stood, and saw that my face-down girl stretched long against the bed, her face still buried in the mattress. The stretch allowed the sheet and her shorts to slip just a bit, just enough to show a small feather tat on the top of her right ass cheek. Emily didn't seem the tattoo type. Hmm.

Turning, I headed into the bathroom to piss and try to start and resolve the morning.

CHAPTER TWO

EMILY

The very last thing I could remember about last night was sitting on the back stoop of O'Gallaghers, bawling.

My life just went from shitty to shittier.

I don't suppose it was really all that bad, but after working a double at O'Gallaghers, I had raced home so I could study for my first major test in my nursing lecture course, only to find out I misplaced my keys somewhere during my walk home.

After starting at O'Gallaghers, I did indeed get rid of my car. Between not having television or a car, and working doubles at O'Gallaghers, I'd been able to afford school and something more than ramen and Kraft Macaroni Dinners. I splurged on Shapes though, because yeah, they were better than the Original.

I would cut out the internet expense too, but I needed that for school.

Anyway, I got home at one in the morning only to discover I hadn't grabbed my keys in my hurry to get a few hours in of studying. I had been planning on studying until two, sleeping until nine, then going to my review with Conor and Rory, before finally heading to class. Everything worked out in my head.

I should have freaking known better. Nothing ever worked as planned.

I got home, couldn't get in, and had to turn back to the pub. Unfortunately, by the time I got back, Rory had already locked up. Having no place to go, I sat on the back stoop, put my head in my hands, and cried.

Cut corners, and eventually they bite you in the ass...and I'm pretty sure mine just did.

So, that was the last of what I remembered.

Somehow, though, I ended up in a bed. I started to come to when the body I had thrown myself against started to move, but it wasn't until the body moved and I could hear someone peeing in a nearby bathroom that I opened my eyes and looked around.

The bedroom was huge. I frowned.

Why was I in a bedroom?

Frantically, I looked down to reassure myself I was in my clothes.

I was.

Thank the good Lord.

What happened though?

I turned around and sat up, rubbing my hand over my face and then looked around the room for a clock.

Ten.

Shit!

Ten!

I was due to meet Rory and Conor like... now!

I scrambled out of the bed and looked around for shoes, spotting them tossed carelessly at the foot of the bed. I pulled myself to stand and just as I was about to slip my feet into my well-worn Birkenstock sandals that had been a gift...

Rory O'fucking-Gallagher came walking out of the bathroom.

Oh my God.

Oh my flipping God.

I spent the night in Rory O'Gallagher's bed.

I threw my body over his. Ok, just my leg, but oh my God, my leg touched something on him!

I swallowed hard, staring at him as he stood in the doorway of what must have been the bathroom. He stood there, all hard body, messy reddish-brown hair, with a delicious morning shadow.

And smirking.

The ass.

"What," he finally said. "No thank you?"

I snapped my head up to look at him from across the room. "For what?" Just like that, he had the ability to piss me off.

"Oh, I don't know," he said, leaning against the doorjamb with his arms crossed over his bare chest, and his legs crossed at the ankles. Everything about him just screamed cocky.

Over-confident.

Asshole.

"Saving your ass last night?" he finished.

I stood straight and started to chew on my thumbnail as I replayed the night prior. "I just remember coming back and sitting on the stoop when I realized you had locked up already," I said, lifting my chin in the air. I wasn't going to tell him I bawled my eyes out.

"Yeah, you fucking fell asleep on the stoop." Rather than anger though, he sounded... Concerned?

Rory O'Gallagher, concerned? Psh. No. Never. That didn't fit his MO.

"Why did you come back?" Still, he stood there, ever so patiently. We didn't have time for this! I had a review with him and Conor, as well as a test that I was likely going to fail at this point.

If I failed this class, I was done. This wasn't me being dramatic; it was the school's rules. I'd be damned if I worked this hard for this long, only to fail one class in the end.

"I don't have time for this," I finally responded, heading toward the bedroom door. I'd see myself out.

"Em." He must have moved from the doorjamb, because I could hear him padding after me. "Emily."

Ignoring him, I reached for the doorknob of what I assumed

was to the stairwell leading down to O'Gallaghers, but before I could pull it open, Rory caged me in against the door. I rested my forehead against the wood and squeezed my eyes shut.

I was going to fail my class.

Not only that, but Conor was likely downstairs and he'd see me leaving the apartment with his brother and, oh my God, if I lost this job, I would really be paddling up shit creek.

"You're a smart girl, Emily," Rory stated to my back.

Ha. Smart girl. Right.

That's why it took me this long to get where I was. Look at the prime example behind me. The guy who made six figures by the time he was twenty. If anyone was smart, it was Rory. Even if he didn't get his money by being a PhD in something extraordinary, he was at least smart in his entrepreneur ways.

"You know better than to sleep outside—behind a bar, no less. Why did you come back?"

I could continue to ignore him. It's what I did best, anyway. And besides, why was he being so...not-Rory-like right now?

Then he really surprised me by grabbing my arm gently and turning me around to face him. I leaned back against the door, defeated, and looked up the minimal inches to stare directly into Rory's green eyes.

I had never noticed how pretty they were before. They were a rich emerald green with an even darker ring around them. His left eye had a slight bright blue speck in it, taking up about a quarter of the bottom of his iris. Add to that his thick, long black eye lashes, and he really was beautiful up close.

He lifted a brow over one of those beautiful eyes, wordlessly urging me to answer him.

"I left my keys here."

Rory frowned now. "What do you mean, you left your keys here? I saw you leave. How'd you get home?"

That was the other thing.

I don't think any of the O'Gallaghers knew I didn't have a

car.

"I walked," I answered honestly, jutting my chin up and preparing myself mentally for Rory's response. We may not get along, he may be a cocky asshole, but one thing the O'Gallaghers were was protective of the people who worked for them.

When one of the barmaids was continuously harassed by a customer and it started to affect her outside of the pub, the boys helped her file a restraining order. When Matt's, one of the weekday bartenders, kid fell ill, only to learn he had a genetic disorder, the O'Gallaghers set up a benefit for his family and the expenses they were starting to see.

Conor did these things because beneath his cocky exterior, he was truly a big softy, something that was painfully evident when you saw him with his baby boy, Aiden. Talk about exploding ovaries. Pair that with how much he loved his girlfriend, Mia, and you couldn't help but fully take in what those closest to him meant to Conor.

As for Rory? I'm sure it was an image thing.

The look of disbelief that passed over his face now would have been comical if it weren't for the fact I was mentally exhausted about how my day was already going.

"At one in the morning? You walked. You're fucking kidding me, right?"

I ground my molars. "No, I'm not fucking kidding you, Rory. I walked. I don't have a car. I walked home like I do every night, just like I walk here every day. I was too busy thinking about a test I have to take today and didn't realize I left my keys here until I got home. Therefore, I had to turn around. But by the time I got back, you had already locked up."

"Emily, you don't walk home at one in the morning around here!"

"It's a decent neighborhood, Rory."

"Yeah, with a couple bars in either direction and therefore, shady as shit people. How long have you not had a car?"

"A year," I grumbled.

"You've worked for us for a year." His voice was eerily calm, as if he was working up a good mad.

I turned my head, avoiding his gaze. Yep, that's right, Rory O'Gallagher.

"You mean to tell me. You have walked here and back. At least four times a week. For a fucking year?"

I snaked my arms between us so I could cross them under my chest, and tilted my head to the side, sighing heavily. "Rory, I have places to go and things to do, so let's not continue this. You don't really care anyway. Thank you for the place to sleep, even though I wish you would have just woken me up. I'm sorry for...anything I may have done in my sleep." My words came out cold, but that seemed to be my only temperature where Rory was concerned. I thought back to the erection my leg brushed against and I felt my face flush.

Maybe there was some intermixing heat in there, too.

My eyes quickly glanced down to be sure he wasn't up any longer. That would be so, so awkward right now.

But.

Nope.

Oh my God. Oh my God, Rory had a boner and he was talking to me while almost holding me up against the door and it was much too late in the game to be considered morning wood any longer.

Oh. My. God.

There was a new panic stirring in me, fighting over the panic of the fact my future was about to go down the drain incredibly fast because I was going to fail my class.

"Oh that?" Rory chuckled, this time his own voice cold, before looking down and grabbing himself. I fought against the gasp.

"Natural, baby." He squeezed himself and let out a groan, biting his lip. His eyelids dropped, his gaze heavy, as he kept his eyes locked on mine.

He was so...so...crude.

I turned and pushed against him to try and get the door open, my butt pushing back into him. I nearly jumped out of my skin with the feel of his hardness against me.

Finally, he stepped back and I swung the door open, scrambling down the stairs without looking back.

CHAPTER THREE

RORY

I chuckled to myself as Emily ran down the stairs, her messy white blonde hair billowing behind her as she made her hasty exit.

When she reached the bottom, she glanced back up the stairs and caught me watching her. Her face scrunched up in a disgusted frown, her brows drawn together—her lips puckered angrily, too—and she pushed through the door to the kitchen.

God, she was so fucking easy to get going.

I stepped back into the apartment and closed the door, needing to put on clothes before meeting Emily and Conor downstairs. I made my way back to the bedroom and glanced at my bed, remembering the feel of Emily, all soft and warm, next to me. The room smelled like sex and I found myself kind of wishing it had been Emily earlier in the night, instead of Cute Halter Girl.

I started my night with a boner and one cute girl, and ended the sleeping hours even harder, with Emily's snark and sass filling my head. She was so cold all the time, that just once I wanted to feel her, see her, all hot and bothered.

By this time, I knew that Emily would have entered Conor's office. He was bound to ask her about her attire. Emily was the type who was always made up. When she wasn't in her ass-hugging jeans or sexy short-shorts with an O'Gallagher's shirt, she was in a sundress or nice jeans with an even nicer top. Her hair was always done and her face always made up.

Conor would probably be shocked to see her in her after-work clothes, messy-assed hair, and makeup smeared face.

He'd ask her about it. She wouldn't lie. I didn't think the girl knew how to lie, she was that fucking pure and genuine.

Which made her obvious distaste of me so incredibly true and real. From the moment I met her, I knew she didn't like me.

"Rory, this is Emily," Conor said from his desk as I stepped into the back office prior to a shift. I preferred to do more of the behind-the-scenes marketing aspects of running the pub, but lately I was working behind the bar more than usual. "I hired her to fill some of the holes on the floor and she'll likely do some closings, too." Sitting across from Conor was a gorgeous blonde with clear blue eyes, eyes I could probably find myself lost in. Her hair was down and over a shoulder, showing off its thickness while the light played off the light blonde hues, making it appear almost white.

In my quick perusal, I didn't notice any tattoos, no necklaces, no bracelets. She did wear a pair of simple diamond-like studs in her ears, but other than that...

She was a complete blank canvas.

I stepped closer and offered my hand. "Rory O'Gallagher." I flashed a grin at her, wanting to win her over. Fuck, I'd give up a week's worth of easy pussy for one night with this one here.

The sweet, genuine smile she had on her face when I walked in changed just slightly, but in the direction of cold rather than warm. "I've heard of you." She offered her hand and I tried my damnedest to ignore Conor's smirk-y chuckle. "Emily Winters."

I took her hand in mine, trying to ignore the coldness of her smile, but when our hands touched for only the merest of seconds, she slipped her hand from mine and turned back to Conor, promptly dismissing me.

What the actual fuck?

At that moment, I decided that Winters was the perfect

surname for her. Not only was her hair the color of winter, but she was just as cold.

From then on, I spent my few moments with her riling her up and she took the opportunities to send subtle jabs my way, things like I "whored myself for money" and that I stole from the poor.

Subtle like that, yeah?

Whatever she'd heard about me had to have been slightly exaggerated. I certainly didn't whore myself for money, but I would definitely admit to sleeping around. And I definitely didn't steal from the poor. Convincing people of where to spend their money was a gift, and it wasn't my fault that some people didn't pay attention to their own bottom lines.

I shook my head. I had things to do and sitting here reminiscing about Emily and whatever she thought were my wrong-doings wasn't going to get my day going.

Thankfully, my cock decided that thinking about Emily wasn't a good idea and I was able to change comfortably into my favorite pair of Left Field NYC jeans, pairing it with a well-worn Henley shirt. I ran my hand through my unkempt hair, splashed on a dash of cologne because any more and Conor would send me to the showers—the dickwad—and brushed my teeth quickly before heading down to face the firing squad that was my brother.

By the time I got to the office, Emily was standing and smiling for Conor—the ass—and Conor was laughing at something she said. Apparently Conor gave her the news we were giving her a raise. She was due for one and besides, she was a good employee and deserved therefore deserved it. Then he handed her a pair of keys.

I frowned and caught the last part of their conversation, standing just outside the door while neither caught on to my presence.

"—I'll return it in three hours tops."

"Don't worry about it. Keep it for the rest of the school week. My bike is still in the back if Mia needs me for anything today."

Emily frowned, but not like the frowns she gave me. This was more of a concerned one. "But if Mia needs you for anything, she can't very well get on the bike! And what about Aiden?"

"You just worry about passing your test, Em. We'll be fine here."

She worried on her lip and glanced around the room in what I had learned was her way of trying to come up with an alternative to whatever was being said. Unfortunately, I wasn't quick enough to pushing away from the door and her eyes locked on to mine.

And yep. There it was.

That quick look of disdain in my direction.

Fighting the urge to roll my eyes and shake my head, I stepped into the room. Even Conor's open face turned to one of scorn. Fuck, I couldn't do anything right with anyone today.

"Rory. You're late."

"I overslept. I was busy rescuing damsels last night." I winked in Emily's direction and earned myself the scowl I knew was coming.

"Emily, you can go," Conor said kindly to her. "You don't need to stick around for Rory's ass-whoopin'."

Emily laughed—she fucking laughed—at Conor before moving around the desk to give my big, burly brother a hug. When she moved to step past me, I turned sideways to allow her through. She turned as well, making sure to leave a fucking-assed huge gap between our bodies.

"Watch out for sleeping bodies on the back stoop!" I yelled after her as she headed toward the back door. Emily didn't even bother to turn, instead just giving me the bird over her shoulder.

I chuckled and shook my head as I stepped into Conor's office completely.

"Shut the door."

Well, then. Conor meant business today.

Fucker couldn't fire me. I paid for half of this joint, and it was my fucking ingenuity that kept patrons coming in the doors and our asses above the red line.

I shut the door anyhow before moving to sit in the seat Emily had just vacated.

"What's up, big brother?" I sat back casually in the chair, allowing my feet to rest under Conor's desk from my side, my ankles crossed.

"I asked you before Aiden was born if you were going to be able to step up here, but Rory..." He shook his head and ran a hand down his face. "Fuck, Rory, I know you do a lot for the place, but I really need you to be more accountable for your time. I can't fucking rely on you. For your shifts, sure, but this morning? You being late for a fucking meeting with an employee? Regardless of whatever the fuck happened with you two, I need to know that I can count on you for the business side of things. Fuck, Rory, I'd love it if I could cut back another day but I can't do that if you aren't going to be reliable."

I crossed my arms over my chest and feigned indifference. "It was just a review meeting with Emily. Fuck, I already knew we were giving her a raise; what the fuck did you need me here for?"

"To do the fucking review, Rory!" Conor roared. It wasn't very often that my big brother lost his cool; he was pretty laid back in that regard, but obviously something was stressing the big guy. "If I can't fucking rely on you to do business ended things when I can't be here, who the fuck can I rely on?"

"Allow Brenna to buy in," I shrugged a shoulder, essentially dismissing Conor's concern. Sure, Brenna never showed an interest in the business side of the bar, but hell, it was her namesake, too.

"Always have an answer, don't you? Such a fucking smart ass." Conor leaned forward and shook his head. "Even if Brenna did buy in, she isn't ready for the business side. Fuck, Stone has more knowledge on this end than she does. But that's beside the point. When can I count on you, Rory? When are you going to grow the fuck up and be an adult?"

"Woah-ho-ho," I held my hands up, palms out. "Hold up a second." I sat up straight and pointed at myself. "Me? Me, grow up. Are you fucking shitting me right now, Conor? Look who's fucking talking! Up until Mia showed up fucking five months pregnant, you were just the fuck like me!"

"Yeah, and I owned up to my shit and I grew up. You're fucking twenty-nine years old, Rory."

"And you were thirty-two!" I couldn't believe he was pulling this. "Who the hell comes up with ideas for raising our revenue, huh? Yeah, that's right, fucker. Me," I said, pointing at my chest. "My ideas have allowed you to work the fucking bar three fucking nights a week and do the cushy thing the other four."

"I have a family."

"Yeah, and a woman who won't marry you." As soon as the words left my mouth, I knew I hit the wrong button. Conor's face went blank so fucking fast and his eyes closed down. Fuck me.

Conor pushed away from his desk and grabbed his bike keys from the top drawer. "Just grow the fuck up, Rory." When his voice went from heated to so incredibly cool, I knew that it wasn't going to be easy to get back in my brother's good graces again. It was going to take a little bit longer than an hour run on his bike.

"Look, Con—"

"I hope I can trust you to open the damn bar on time." Without another word, Conor stormed out past me, opening the back door and allowing it to slam shut behind him.

Well shit, that didn't end exactly well.

CHAPTER FOUR

EMILY

When I first started at O'Gallaghers, I would be lying if I said either of the O'Gallagher brothers didn't scare me. Shoot, Brenna even scared me to a degree. She was all sweet but there was definitely more lurking behind her eyes.

But Conor had changed over the last year, all thanks to his girlfriend. Mia took Conor from the womanizing brute he'd been reputed to being, to the type of guy you could easily go to with your problems.

When I entered his office this morning, he took one look at me and told me to sit. I told him everything from the past eight hours and how I was terrified I was going to get kicked out of my program for failing a test—if I failed one, I only had room to fail one more; two times, and you were out—and he offered me the keys to his truck. It was also a relief to know he had been intending to offer me a raise, minimal as it was, but I knew that it would help.

Then, while he didn't scold me, he was pretty firm about the fact that had he known I was walking to and from the bar, he would have offered me the apartment above the bar, not Rory, because "that fucker already had a place." Conor also offered to change my hours around so that I would still be on the floor during peak times, but not so incredibly late that it would interfere with my school schedule and studying. These were all things I'd been too terrified to ask, for fear I'd lose my job. There were more senior barmaids on the team, so it made sense to me that they would have first bill for hours, but knowing that Conor had my best interests in mind definitely helped calm some of my trepidations.

With the benefit of Conor's truck, I managed to get back to my apartment, shower and change, grab my notes and notecards, and fly to the school, where I was then able to cram for an hour before the test. I felt confident going in, and felt even better coming out.

When I returned to O'Gallaghers to thank him, I was surprised to see that Conor's bike was gone. Was something wrong with Mia?

I entered the pub through the back and waved hello to the weekday cook, Mike, on the floor before heading to Conor's office to write a note to say 'thank you.'

When I exited the office, Mike held up a hand as he dropped something in the fryer. "You want something, Em?"

I had nowhere to be and I hadn't eaten yet today. "Sure, what's your special today?" The cooks always worked with the menu Rory and Conor thought up, but were allowed an additional special every day.

"Just homemade mini tacos today," Mike said with a purposeful chuckle. If there was one thing the O'Gallaghers grumbled about with the menu, it was non-American or non-Irish items.

"Ah, deviating from your Cheeseburger Shalaylees." They were the most delicious thing on the menu; ground beef in a wonton wrapper boat, sprinkled with cheese and dipped in a Guinness barbeque sauce. Whenever Mike brought out the mini tacos—which were nearly the same thing, except with spices and sour cream—Conor went on and on about them and about how if he wanted a Mexican version of his menu, he'd change the name of the place.

But Conor and Rory agreed to give the cooks their menu

item and, in all honesty, the main items sold more than the special items.

That, and Conor was a fair guy.

And he liked the mini tacos. I've seen him stuff his face with them a time or two—or twenty.

"I'll do an order of those, sure," I told him, but before I could find a place to sit, Rory came through the kitchen doors.

"I need to talk to you," he said, looking at me but addressing no one in particular. Ass could at least use my name.

He stalked past me to the back office, assuming I'd follow.

I didn't want to, but he was one of my bosses so on principle, I did.

I noticed it earlier—hell, I noticed it a few times over the year but I really appreciated it now—but the way Rory wore jeans that molded to his ass, making it mouth-watering, and the white long-sleeved Henley that still showed off the groves of his shoulders and back, further adding to his appeal. Where Conor was big and bulky in muscle, Rory had more of a swimmer's body—but was definitely still well-endowed in the muscle department.

Rory only stood a few inches taller than me, but his muscle gave me that odd sense of security.

Which was incredibly disconcerting, seeing as I didn't much like the guy.

When I entered the office, I deliberately left the door open but Rory took my wrist in his hand and pulled me from the door, shutting it one handedly. Before I could open my mouth about him manhandling me, I was pushed against the door and his mouth was on mine.

I opened my mouth and put my hands to his chest with the intent to pull away and tell him to stop, but instead I brushed my tongue against his probing one. My hands moved up and were in his two-months-past-due hair, fisting against the locks and holding his face to mine. My eyes were closed but I could feel him all around me, one hand on the side of my neck, curling over the back, and the other grabbing my hip, keeping me pulled close.

I hated him but, oh my God, the way he kissed. The way he took control of my body.

What in the ever loving hell was I doing? And why did I enjoy it so much?

I wanted to hate him. This was the man who dated women long enough to get them to leave raving reviews for O'Gallaghers, only to dump them twenty-four hours later.

This was the man who pretended to support his community, only to be a twelve-year old ass about it later, leaving terrible reviews and slandering the other companies.

This was the man who participated in those stupid pyramid schemes for weight loss companies, supporting the fit and beautiful, only to push down and be cruel to those who didn't fit in with his ideal.

Rory's social media presence was everywhere and in it, he went on and on about how sometimes making money took time, that being an entrepreneur took patience, and how every single person had something to offer, but his actions were always so incredibly different from his words.

These were the very reasons I didn't like him.

He was a fake.

He was a fraud.

He was an asshole.

But my God, he kissed me like he wanted me.

I had to remind myself that this was simply him.

This was Rory O'Gallagher at his finest.

I needed to push away. I needed to put us back on our even ground.

Instead, I pulled him closer. I was going to hate myself in ten minutes, but I was going to enjoy him for the time being.

CHAPTER FIVE

I was through with Emily Winters spitting nails at me.

I wanted her fire and fury utilized in a different way, and damn if she wasn't proving she could hand it out in spades.

I'd been wiping down the bar while one of our newer bartenders, Jordan, manned the bar itself, when I heard her voice coming from the kitchen.

I'd always been drawn to her voice, even though whenever she used it for me it was cold. I could pull her voice out of a rambunctious crowd, always able to pin-point her by following the melodic notes in her tone.

For the second time that day, it was ice cold Emily Winters who gave me a raging hard-on. The morning wood didn't count but when I held her against the door? That was all her, no matter what I told her.

So when I heard her voice, when her voice gave me this new reaction, I knew I wasn't about to let her get away. I would take everything she gave me, and turn it into a passion burning so bright she wouldn't know what hit her. She wouldn't remember why she hated me.

Her hands were in my hair, her mouth fighting mine for control, and I was in fucking seventh heaven. Her willowy body molded against mine in a way that made me want to keep her close. Her hips lined up perfectly to mine and when she lifted her leg to wrap around my hip, opening her groin up to fit snug against mine, I had to stop myself from grinding into her, pushing her even further into the door.

Blindly, I stumbled for the double locks on the office door.

I walked in on Mia and Conor once. What I saw burned my retinas. Sweet Mia had a dirty side, and I would never be able to get that image out of my head.

There wasn't any way in hell someone was walking in on Emily and me.

Unfortunately, my actions caused Emily to apparently fall back into the present, because with her hands still fisted in my hair, she pulled my head back and stared at me, mouth open, chest heaving as she fought for air.

She stared.

And stared.

And stared some more. It was a little unnerving.

Still, I didn't break the silence. I wanted her with my entire fucking being and I wasn't about to let my mouth run and have her run in response.

I expected her backlash. To be honest, I expected a knee in the nuts.

I didn't get either.

"Once."

"Once?" I repeated, my eyes searching hers and dropping to her mouth. She licked her lips before continuing, making me groan out loud.

"One time, Rory O'Gallagher. And then I'm going back to hating you."

Not giving her room to change her mind, I grabbed her ass and hoisted her up, pulling her clothed pussy close to my hard cock as she wrapped both legs around me. She lowered her mouth back to mine as I made my way to the couch.

I rearranged my hands so one cupped her ass, freeing my other to grab my wallet from my back pocket. I tossed it down on the couch as I sat, and when she rolled her hips over me, I moaned into her mouth. Fucking heaven.

I wanted my hands on her skin, all over her body. I quickly pulled her shirt up and off over her head, our mouths parting for only the mere seconds it get rid of the garment. Her mouth immediately fused back to mine, her tongue sliding swiftly against my own. I wasn't able to truly appreciate the fact that she didn't wear a bra, but my hands quickly found purchase against her slight chest.

Emily was built like a dancer, willowy and toned. She was tall, but everything else on her was small. Her hips. Her waist. Her tits.

But her little nipples were rock hard against my palms as I rolled them. I slid my hands down so I could pluck at the taut peaks, rolling them simultaneously between my index fingers and thumbs. Emily's groin rolled against mine in time to her little mewls of pleasure, all muffled by my mouth.

I squeezed one of her nipples hard enough to have her rip her mouth from mine. She moaned out loud, her head dropping back, exposing the long column of her neck to me. I leaned in, scraping my lower teeth against her skin and sucked in a kiss right below her chin. I released some of the pressure my fingers had on her, gently rolling the nubs once again.

Moving my mouth, I pressed kisses up her jawline and toward her ear. I sucked her earlobe into my mouth, my tongue playing against the stud she wore there before I gently bit down. Her body shuddered against mine and I felt as she moved her legs, her knees pressing harder into my hips.

I wished she were still in her cotton shorts from earlier so I could feel her heat, feel her wetness pooling against me. Fuck, I wish she'd changed into one of her summer dresses instead of these jeans, as great as they looked on her. My hand itched to palm her bare ass. Instead, I settled with holding her hip, my thumb rubbing gently over her hip bone.

Her hair was in her signature ponytail, and I wrapped the

long tresses around my other hand, pulling back lightly so I could move my mouth from her neck, to her ear, to her chest. I pressed a kiss over her sternum, between the slight mounds that made up her chest, before traveling over to her tit. I opened my mouth, but rather than suck her into my mouth, rather than devour her little pink, hard nipple, I gave her slow lick.

The feel of her against my tongue...not a word to describe it.

Emily's moan, the sigh that ran through her body, was long and drawn out.

I moved to her other nipple and licked her there too, slower this time. I felt her stomach quiver against my thumb and I just fucking knew she was going to come.

All from a little action on her tits.

I moved back to the first nipple, licking it once more before flicking my tongue over it quickly. Her hips began their restless movement against mine, her body seeking release. Her breathing became heavier, her hands in my hair tightening more.

Her breaths were coming out in quick little pants, her mewls sounding around the room. Quicker, I flicked my tongue until finally I gave her the release she was looking for and I bit, ever so gently, on the peak.

Emily's knees drew up against my sides and her body straightened, pushing impossibly close to my face, as she came.

Fucking damn.

I grinned against her chest, letting go of her nipple and pressing a kiss to the side of her lips, her mouth open as she fought the release taking over her body. I sucked on her lower lip, her body still shuddering.

I kept my eyes on her closed ones, willing them to open so I could see the heat behind the cool blue depths.

C'mon, Em... Open those eyes...

When she did, her pupils were dilated and her nostrils flared with her gasps of breath. Her face was flushed and damn if I hadn't ever seen a more beautiful woman in the throes of passion.

CHAPTER SIX

EMILY

I should really hate myself right now.

I totally just came all over Rory's lap like any number of the girls he convinced to sleep with him. But, my God, I wanted more.

Rory O'Gallagher was addicting

If this was how he was with his lady friends after he turned on the charm, I could totally see why the girls lined up to sit on his cock, even knowing he'd leave them sooner than later.

I needed to remember who Rory was outside of sex, but I would get back to that thought later. Right now, I wanted my hands on his skin and his hard cock between our bodies.

To start.

My breath was still trembling out of my parted lips and I could feel my pussy pulsing from the ebbing release, but I was ready to move this on to the next step.

His hands were still on my hips and he didn't seem to be in any sort of hurry to get naked.

So I was going to fix that.

I reached down to pull up on the hem of his Henley shirt, my eyes fixed on his body as I exposed his tan, muscle-filled flesh. As I cleared the middle of his chest, I wasn't all that surprised to find he was bare of hair.

He probably waxed.

Or had it removed by a laser.

Pushing the negative thoughts about him out of my head, I

continued to pull his shirt up until finally, Rory got with the program and reached behind his head, removing the shirt completely.

I put my hands on his bare chest, taking a brief moment to drink him in. His normally messy hair was made even worse by my hands, and he still wore the shadow on his cheeks and chin from this morning. I briefly wondered what the stubble would feel like on my lady bits.

My body shivered involuntarily over him, which only caused a grin to spread over Rory's features.

Not wanting him to open his mouth with some arrogant comment, ruining the moment, I busied my hands with the fly of his designer jeans. They probably cost the same as one of my classes alone.

I hurriedly unbuttoned the fly, reaching in to pull his hardened cock free of his jeans and briefs. Needing some sort of upper hand, I gingerly rubbed my thumb along the ridge of its head, before moving off his lap to kneel between his legs, my hand never leaving his shaft.

I glanced up at him to gauge his reaction. He moved his arms so they spanned the back of the couch, giving him a look of complete and utter comfort.

Like this was an everyday occurrence.

Then again, it probably was.

Willing girl on her knees between his own, angling his cock toward her mouth.

I really had to get out of my head before this entire thing took a sour turn.

I lifted up on my knees, letting my elbows rest easily on his thighs, before enclosing the head of his cock with my mouth. Just the tip.

Just enough so that when I sucked against him, I could revel in the tightening of his thighs under my arms.

Just enough so that when I added light teasing with my

tongue, I could hear his breathy groan above me.

I pulled off him and tilted my head to the side, allowing me to run my tongue up his length without teeth getting in the way and once I reached his head once again, I dropped my mouth, sucking him back deep. My hand grasped him low on his shaft and I added quick, short pumping movements at the base of him.

I pulled back, sucking with all I was worth, ever so slowly, my fist slowing but lengthening its pumping. I felt more than saw as Rory adjusted his ass on the couch.

This time, when I bobbed on the upper half of his length, my palm working the lower half, his hips tightened and he began thrusting up into my mouth, further working my actions against him.

Rory's hands dropped beside him on the couch and from the corner of my eye, I saw as he lifted his hand, moving it toward my head, before dropping it back beside him.

His fingers clenched into the leather cushion of the couch, all while I worked him over, loving the sounds this man was making above me.

He let out a long groan before moving his hands toward my head again, only this time he threaded his hands into my hair. His long fingers cradled the back of my head and I could feel my ponytail loosening.

His hands tightened before he pulled back on my head, surprising me. I honestly would have figured he'd be the guy to hold a girl's head down as he thrust relentlessly into the back of her throat, paying no attention to her gagging.

...and part of me was secretly upset that I didn't experience the unabashed side of Rory.

I allowed him to pull me back but of course I had to make it hard for him by squeezing and sucking him, his cock finally leaving my mouth with a resounding pop.

"God, no more," he groaned. "I'm about to fucking come. Goddamn, Emily." He let go of my head and I could feel how loose my ponytail had gotten. I reached up to just pull the damn thing out.

As he stood, he pulled me up to stand as well and moved me aside so he could quickly shuck his pants and briefs. I quickly lost my own jeans and panties, excited for this to continue.

He reached for me again as he sat, pulling me to him, guiding me to straddle him. His hands palmed my ass.

"You have a tattoo," he said as his hands kneaded me.

Not what I was expecting him to say. I frowned and looked over my shoulder; how had he seen it anyway?

"The other morning," he answered, as if I spoke the question out loud.

"Oh." Still, I frowned. What was with the question? He was hard and throbbing between our bodies; I was wet and hot, waiting to sink onto him. Why was he holding back?

"What's it mean?"

"That I was twenty and drunk and wanted something small." I shook my head. "What's with the questions?"

"Just curious," he answered, reaching for my hair and pulling it over my shoulder. Then he winked. "Needed to recharge a second." There was that Rory I knew and...well, I knew.

With my hair over my shoulder, the length brushed over my erect nipples. The slight feathery feeling had me moaning, but that was quickly changed to a lustful groan as Rory angled my hips so his cock rubbed deliciously against my folds.

Apparently the feeling was nearly too much for him as well. He groaned and squeezed his eyes shut against the feeling.

With a crooked smile on my face, I rubbed over him again. I bit my lip, absolutely loving the feeling of his thick girth between my pussy lips. I couldn't wait to feel him inside me.

I continued to roll my hips against him, my grin fading as my breath quickened and my brows drew in. The ridges of Rory's cock running over my pussy, my clit being rubbed deliciously by his velvety shaft, was almost too much. I let go of my lip as I closed my eyes, my hands finding purchase on his shoulders and I let my head drop back.

His hands were on my hips, his fingers flexing against me, and I nearly jumped from my skin when I felt his lips against the column of my throat once again. Between my grinding against him and the pull of his lips and teeth against my neck, I was ready to come again.

Rory's hips were flexing up under me, thrusting his cock against my folds. He wasn't even in me and this was the best damn sex I had in my sexual history. No wonder he had a reputation.

No wonder girls would do just about anything to be with him and didn't seem to care when he dropped them like yesterday's bad news.

Suddenly, Rory's hands tightened against my sides, his fingers biting painfully into my hips. I lifted my head to search his face.

"Stop. Stop, we gotta stop. I'm gonna fucking come." His voice was thick and the veins in his neck popped as tension wracked his body. "Need to be in you. Fuck, Emily, I need to be inside you."

He loosened his hold on me and shifted me back slightly, just enough that I could feel the cool air filtering between our bodies. Rory reached over for his wallet, quickly flipping it open and pulling out a condom.

I watched as he expertly ripped it open, sheathing himself in a quick downward motion, and pulled me back to him. I lifted up as he angled his covered cock with one hand, his other hand at my lower back.

I put my hands back on his shoulders and sank down on his hardness slowly, my eyes closing at the feelings of complete bliss as my body stretched to accommodate him.

"Fuck. God, fuck!" Rory was saying, well before I fully took him in my body.

I still had a small ways to go but Rory took care of that by thrusting upward into me forcefully. "Fuck. God-fucking-damn, you feel so—"

And then he let out a long groan, his hips bucking under me twice before pushing into me once and holding still.

I could feel him throbbing inside me, but more than just excited throbbing. This was the full deal, pulsing and throbbing.

Were you..?

Did he..?

"Are you serious right now?" I asked, opening my eyes. I was sure disbelief was all over my face.

He fucking came.

For all his sexual prowess, all the women who courted him, he fucking came and we hadn't even truly started!

Rory's face was squeezed tight, the frown between his brows was definitely more than just from his relief, because when the rest of his features relaxed, the creases remained and he squeezed his eyes shut more. "This is so fucking embarrassing."

I wanted to cry.

My body was strung tight and need coursed through my body. I wanted to come around his cock; I wanted his thickness to be the instigator to my orgasm, because there was something about being filled to the brink when you came that really pushed an orgasm through the body.

My eyes never left Rory's closed face, needing for this to be a joke. Maybe he was one of those guys who could cut off their orgasm, splitting it into two or more.

Surely this wasn't over.

This was a one-time thing, and if this was the end of it...

Rory's eyes finally opened, the green orbs looking straight into my own eyes. His pupils were dilated but the look in them was weary. "I am so sorry."

CHAPTER SEVEN

RORY

I finally get into her tight body, and I fucking come.

Even my first time ever, I had more fucking finesse and control over my orgasm. How in the hell did I just...lose my load the moment her pussy started to take me in?

I mean, I held back. The first two inches of her sinking on me.

But it was all gone from there.

It was so fucking embarrassing.

"It's ok," Emily said, her face starting to shut down. She lifted off of me, my slackening cock sliding from her wet, warm sheath. She stood and I watched as the cold front that was Emily Winters fell back into place.

This had been well on its way to my best lay and I had to go and be a prepubescent teenager with his first pussy.

"God, this is embarrassing," I said again, letting my head fall back onto the couch while I pressed my fingers into my eyes. I could hear as Emily sifted through clothes on the floor and decided to man up and open my eyes, only to see her bent forward, her long hair shielding nearly every part of her body as she worked on getting her panties back on.

With a sigh, I took off the condom and stood to discard it, thinking twice before putting it in Conor's waste basket.

But because I was already on his shit list, I moved to the small powder room attached to the office and disposed of it in there.

When I got back into the office, Emily was already in her jeans and had her arms behind her back as she was putting her bra back on. Completely nude still, I moved behind her to try and help her, but she stepped away from me.

Still, she said nothing.

With a heavy sigh and no idea what to say besides 'I'm sorry' or 'I'm embarrassed' yet again, I moved to my own clothes and started to pull them on. Emily had just reached for her shirt when I broke the silence. "You want to do dinner, maybe later tonight?"

I had to do something to make up for this. Shit, I had to try and find a way back in her pants so I could get a do-over.

"No, Rory." She shook her head and pulled her shirt back on. When she pulled her long hair from the collar, letting it fall down her back, I nearly groaned aloud. Damn, I loved her hair.

No sooner than I thought it though, she was pulling it back and up high in a knot that sat at the top of her head. Now I couldn't even watch the locks swaying as she walked away.

I quickly finished dressing and ran a hand through my own hair.

"It's just dinner, Em."

"Yeah, and I said this," she waved a finger in a circle in the space between us, "was a one-time deal." Yep, Ice Cold Emily was back.

Shit, I definitely preferred her hot and bothered over this ice queen persona she did so incredibly well.

I sat on the couch to slip my shoes back on, my finger nearly getting stuck behind my heel as I stepped down in a hurry. Emily was heading toward the door. I hopped up and bounded across the room to reach her before she could pull the door open.

"Dinner," I said again, my lips brushing against the back of her head.

She didn't bother turning toward me. Still facing the door,

she shook her head, her hair brushing my lips as she did so. "No, Rory."

I refrained from dropping my forehead to the back of her head, instead stepping back and allowing her to open the door.

This wasn't over.

Oh no.

It was far from over.

I was just going to let her think she won.

Because Rory O'Gallagher didn't lose.

CHAPTER EIGHT

EMILY

That entire next week, every day I worked at O'Gallaghers Rory was there.

No, not working. We rarely worked together.

Oh no. He was there, seeking me out.

Couldn't the guy just take a hint and go? I told him that sex between us was a one-time deal and while yeah, sure, we didn't actually get to complete the deed—at least, I didn't—what was done was done. I gave in to my moment of weakness where he was concerned and I was finished.

Maybe it had been gratitude for him giving me a bed to sleep in the night before, or maybe it was just me being stupid and wanting to see Rory's charm turned to me, but I gave in and did dirty things with the one person I said I'd never let near me.

And now he wouldn't leave me alone!

Oh, he wasn't annoying or obnoxious about it, not really.

But he was there. Throwing those sly, cocky smiles my way. Leaning in toward me while I was at the bar giving one of the bartenders an order.

And damn, the man smelled wonderful.

He started to keep the stubble look, which only allowed my mind to wander to those dirty thoughts of what it would feel like on the more sensitive areas on my body. He started to pull his hair back into a stubby pony tail and I had to say, the long hair, man-bun look never did anything for me but good God, Rory was fucking gorgeous and pulled it off so damn well.

I clenched my jaw against the thoughts, trying to redirect my mind elsewhere.

You know, to things that were important.

Like my next test. Or, more presently, the order Stone just slid my way to deliver.

I grabbed the two glasses and lone bottle, putting them on my tray, all while avoiding Rory's gaze on me. I deliberately turned in the direction away from him in order to deliver the drinks, praying for another table to flag me down. Something for a little more time away from Rory.

My prayers were answered when I heard my name over the music.

"Emily."

I glanced toward the sound and saw that Conor had just walked into the pub from the front door. He was heading toward the back but looked over at me and waved me back. "Let's talk."

Assuming it had something to do with the truck I was borrowing, I delivered the drinks and hurried back to the front. Placing my tray in its home spot, I still managed to avoided Rory.

"Talking to Con, Stone," I told him as he poured another lager.

"Got it." Stone flashed his eyes toward me momentarily while completing his task, letting me know it was me he was talking to.

I could feel Rory's eyes on me as I walked through the swinging kitchen door, until the door swung shut behind me. With a relieved sigh, I walked down the kitchen and around the corner to the office.

Conor was just sitting down, closing a desk drawer he must have dropped his bike key into.

"How's everything going with school?" he asked as I stepped into the room. When I moved to sit on the couch, I fought a blush as the memories of the last time I was in this office flooded my mind.

"Good. I passed my test last week by a few points, but I think I'll be good. Did you need the truck back?"

Conor stretched back in his chair, slouching some and crossing his arms over his chest. "You can keep it for a bit longer. Mia and I were talking and she came up with an alternative. You can absolutely say no, but I want to start out by telling you this isn't a gift. I know you have pride and we don't want to step on toes."

I sat up straight, a frown deepening on my face. "Ok?"

"Mia and I want to help get you into a car of your own. I know you said you couldn't do the payments right now, and I completely respect that. You're only a semester out and while I don't want to think about the fact I'm close to losing one of my better barmaids," he said this last part with a grin, "I know that your plan is to do nursing. If you're afraid of your credit, I can co-sign on the loan. Either way, Mia and I can help cover payments until you're on your feet and you can pay us back."

I nibbled on my lower lip. This was a phenomenal deal and I'd be silly to pass it up but...

"I don't like the idea of owing you." I shifted in my seat only to sit up taller. "It is incredibly generous of you guys though. Thank you."

"Just take the damn car."

My head flew in the direction of the door. I didn't see it open, but standing there, leaning against the jamb in the way Rory tended to do, was the man himself. How long had he been standing there? How much did he hear? Certainly enough for him to tell me to take what Conor and Mia were offering.

I felt my face flush. This time, it had nothing to do with the two of us in this very room but with mortification. I mean, I knew that Rory knew about my troubles. He was partially my boss, after all. But dealing with Conor was so much easier than Rory, the guy whose achievements made my once upon a time plans look like rubbish simply because I failed and he soared. Pretending that all we had between us was cold distaste, but oddly hot chemistry, was much easier to deal with than the knowledge that this cocky, self-entitled, wealthy guy was well aware of my financial failings.

I shifted again but before I could get a word in edgewise, Rory pushed himself from the frame and entered the room, respectably closing the door behind him.

"It's just a car, Emily. You can't keep walking at one in the fucking morning."

"Conor's changing my schedule," I said as Conor looked at his brother, brow raised over his right eye, and said, "Her schedule is changing."

"That was awesome. Do it again," Rory replied, but with a deadpan expression on his face. "It's like you two practiced that." He walked to the edge of the desk and propped his tight ass on the corner, arms crossed over his chest. While Conor took the slouched, comfortable, welcoming position at his chair, Rory in front of him like he was, was like putting up an invisible wall between Conor and I. Rory demanded my attention and again, I hated myself for wanting to give it to him.

"You want to finish the semester without failing, you need to be better about your time," Rory was saying. I had never seen him take such an authoritative stance when it came to the pub and their employees.

Would it further make me a heel if I said it turned me on a little bit? You know, just a tiny bit.

"You spend, what? Twenty minutes walking here? Another twenty home? If you drove, you'd be cutting off damn near seventy-five percent of that time. That gives you another thirty minutes of study time. So long as you're not cramming it all in one session, that's another great chunk of time to get your brain to focus and to retain everything you're teaching it. I'm willing to bet your scores will improve, from that extra thirty minutes alone."

I glanced over at Conor to see what he was making of all this, but his eyes were on the back of his brother's head and he wore a smirk on his face. Apparently he was amused.

Well, I wasn't.

"I'm doing fine right now. With my hours changing, I have more time in the evening to attend study groups with my peers. My scores on projects have already improved, and it's only been four days."

"You're being obstinate."

That sexual tension I was feeling by his authoritative self?

Yeah.

It was gone.

I couldn't sit up any straighter than I already was, but I refused to get to my feet and close the distance between us. Instead, I screwed up my face in my best bitch face and let it all out, "And you're being an ass. You think you know everything and honestly, you don't. What the hell do you know about studying, Rory? You probably slept with half your teachers in college!"

Conor smothered a chuckle behind his hand.

Rory just gave a menacing smirk. "Yep. It was pretty damn hot, too. Some of the best sex I had until recently." I'm sure it was only because Conor wouldn't catch the movement, but Rory shifted his eyes to the couch beside me before winking at me. "It was pretty much the most exciting sex I'd had, the fear of being caught, you know? But lately…sex has been pretty exciting."

I fought a smirk. Yeah, so exciting he couldn't hold himself back.

"Just take the damn car," he repeated.

"Why do you care?" I could feel my anger deflating. Really, it was exhausting fighting with him. That and I had already been leaning toward accepting Conor's offer.

Rory just stared at me. Not a single emotion crossed his features. His body was still strung tight as he leaned on the desk with his arms crossed. But he stared, and he stared.

"Just take the car," he finally said, pushing himself off the desk. "I'm out. Stone's got the bar." Without waiting for a response from Conor, he left the room, closing the door behind him quietly.

I puffed out my cheeks, waiting for the tension to leave the air. Surely Conor would take that outburst from his brother as more than boss-to-employee concern.

And sure enough—

"You want to tell me what that was about?" But rather than sounding pissed, Conor was...

Amused?

I wiped my palms on my shorts and shook my head. "Nothing. Rory has just decided to turn his non-existent game on to me."

Looking even more amused—if that were possible—Conor grinned crookedly. "Do you want me to do something about it? We don't have a fraternization policy, but if he's bothering you, I can do something."

I sighed. I could end all of this right now. Conor would make sure Rory would leave me alone. I wouldn't have to deal with his advances.

But just at that moment, I could smell his cologne in the air and my pussy clenched involuntarily. Damn body. I mean, what was the deal? I spent a year disliking him and one day, I decide to give in to his charms, he doesn't even finish the deed, and still I wanted him?

I sighed again and shook my head. "No. It's fine. I can handle him."

The look didn't leave Conor's face though. Instead, his grin deepened and he nodded upward once. "Ok." He sat up and uncrossed his arms, leaning into the desk. "But the car. Mia will kill me if I tell her I couldn't talk you into it. Have you seen my woman lately with her hormonal outbursts?"

This time I grinned. Mia was a hoot.

She was sweet and quiet, and honestly, pregnancy did her good. She glowed in the way I often just thought was hooey nonsense. But her temper…

Who'd have thought the Irish one in that relationship would have the calmer disposition?

"Are you afraid of Mia?" I asked, my grin filling.

Conor smirked. "You don't live with her."

Changing the subject off of me, I asked, "Are you guys ready for a second baby? I'm guessing that Aiden doesn't understand."

He was probably too young and, while I was an only child, I could only imagine that the deeper the age gap between babies, the more likely resentment would occur. But at nine and a half months, I was sure Aiden didn't know any different.

"Nah, he's too young," Conor confirmed. "I think it might change after Ava's born though." And unfortunately, Conor wasn't letting me off the hook that easily. "You've only got what, five months until graduation? Take the car, Emily. It'll make Mia feel better."

"Just Mia?"

Conor shook his head, chuckling. "Probably Rory too."

I couldn't stop the growl that resonated in my chest, which only had Conor barking out a laugh. "You two are fucking great to watch." Conor stood and pulled on his jeans. "Good luck, Em."

I took my cue to stand as well and shrugged a shoulder. "There's nothing to watch."

"Sure, keep telling yourself that." Conor walked me to the door, the shit-eating grin on his face still in place. "You're not on the schedule tomorrow. How about you take the truck, pick up Mia, and go find yourself a car. Mia can take the truck home after."

Fully realizing this was a battle I wasn't going to win, I nodded. "Ok. I will. Thank you, Conor." As much as I hated it, I wasn't ungrateful.

We walked back to the bar where I resumed my shift, and Conor sat at the bar, talking with Stone. The rest of my shift flowed easily, probably because everything was starting to fall into place. That and I wouldn't feel terrible if I had their truck and Mia went into labor.

And then there was Rory.

And for the first time since meeting him, his name brought an unwanted smile to my lips.

I'd have to think about that.

CHAPTER NINE

RORY

I may have talked Mia into having something to do when she and Emily were supposed to go car shopping.

Just may have.

I mean, I wasn't the pushy type, so if I admitted to myself that I was finding ways to be in Emily's presence, I would have to double check the status of my man card. The only action my cock had gotten in the last week, since she and I got together—yes, I was choosing to forget the issue I had that day—was from my hand in the shower.

Yesterday in Conor's office, seeing Emily's sass and fire directed at me wasn't anything new, no, but there was a little more passion in her voice. She was weakening toward me and I was going to take full advantage of that.

Starting by hijacking her car shopping trip with Mia.

After checking my email and corresponding with my clients and team members alike, I checked my online back-office for new orders of protein powders and muscle building e-books. I loved the pub, don't get me wrong, but this little side business I had was what truly paid the bills, and had been since I joined the company six years ago.

And I only really paid attention to it once, maybe twice a week.

I went from making a pretty penny with fake IDs and doing the occasional DJ-ing at house parties in college, to making a much shinier one by selling my muscle building knowledge. This day and age, all you needed was a good looking body and an Instagram account, and you could pull anyone in who wanted to look better.

After I printed my latest order sheet, I shut down the computer and headed down to the pub. Mia had planned on Emily meeting her here, so it made the whole, "Mwah-ha-ha, I'm coming with you" ordeal easier to accomplish.

It was early yet, so while the doors were open for business, we only had one customer sitting at the bar. His eyes were glued to one of the televisions, which was only airing the local news. I looked around, unsure of who was working today.

Jordan, a new kid we hired a few weeks ago, took that moment to pop up from whatever he was doing under the bar. Probably dropped something.

The kid was clumsy as fuck, which was the exact reason we were keeping him on the opening rotation for a bit. He was great with the customers and could mix a mean drink—he just had to work on his hands and keeping glasses in them.

"Hey, Jordan. How's it going?" I asked as I rounded the back of the bar, grabbing a bottle of water from the cooler.

"Good." The kid was a bit scrawny but in a hipster kind of way, which actually worked well with the early afternoon crowd. He was working on cutting limes when the front door opened. Expecting it to be Emily, I turned in my stool to see.

Nope.

Brenna and Stone.

Brenna and Stone?

I stepped off my stool and rounded the bar again, water in hand, to look at the schedule. Stone wasn't due to be in until three, but Brenna was Jordan's second man. I was going to shout hello to them but when I turned back toward the open bar area, they were nowhere to be found.

I scanned the bar, my water to my lips, and eventually saw

the two of them in a corner near the dart boards, having a quiet, but seemingly heated, discussion.

Stone was a good guy. So whatever the issue, it wasn't him. Brenna probably lost her temper and was pissed to run into him. If Emily and I had our glaring moments, Brenna and Stone were just the opposite. They both flirted ruthlessly with one another, but then again they both flirted with just about anybody. They were the example of harmless flirting.

I narrowed my eyes.

But what if it wasn't harmless flirting?

Fuck, if Stone was…

Nope.

Wouldn't happen.

I shook my head and chuckled to myself. Stone may not be as obvious in his ways when it came to sex, but the man went out almost nightly. He always had plans with a female. I was pretty sure he was seriously seeing someone, but Stone was quiet about his personal life.

Had been since the moment we hired him.

"Yo, Bren," I shouted over the bar, finally earning their attention.

"What, Rory?" she called out, a bit of bite to her voice, as she crossed her arms and shoved around Stone, walking toward me.

I chuckled, watching as my sister essentially stomped toward the bar. "Leave the poor guy alone. What the hell did he do to you?"

She mumbled something under her breath but before I could have her repeat what she said, Emily came into the pub.

And her hair was down.

And straight.

Fuck me.

Why the hell did Mia get this version of her? What did Mia do to deserve Emily's fucking gorgeous hair down and swaying toward her ass?

Before I could walk toward her though, Stone, the stealthy fucker, managed to end up behind me and slapped my shoulder. "What are you doing here so early on a Saturday?"

I held up a finger and with what had to be a shit-eating grin, I looked toward Emily—who was almost to Stone and me—and lifted my chin as I spoke with her. "You ready to go get a car?"

She stopped, dead in her tracks, and her brows lowered in that way I was sure was reserved for me and me alone. "Where's Mia?"

"Last minute doctor's appointment?" I said but thought better of blowing it off with a shrug. I mean, it didn't matter if she figured out I set today up, but I had to at least get her to go with me before she did.

Because let's be honest, she figures it out and she's walking.

"Yep." I nodded. "Baby Ava's getting ready to join the masses."

Emily's frown deepened. "Why didn't she just call to reschedule? She or Con needs to be there to co-sign if I find a car."

Fuck. She was going to figure this out.

I had to get her in my truck before she did. She was so fucking smart. Nothing got past Emily. I should have been better prepared for this.

"Mia said she or Con would be able to stop by the dealership when you were ready," I said on the spot. I reached out and put my hand on her lower back, guiding her back toward the doors. Behind me, Stone coughed, but I'm pretty sure the asshole was covering a laugh.

Emily stumbled as she walked in the direction I was guiding her. I bit back a groan when she turned her head toward me, which made her hair brushed my forearm. "But—"

"Nope, she wanted to be sure you found a car today. Earlier the better, too, because you know, salesmen get pushy toward the end of the day when they've not met goal. So we need to get you out there early and if we find you something, Mia and Con can meet us and help with the paperwork."

Emily was still frowning but she pushed through the front door willingly. "...Ok."

I was kind of surprised she wasn't putting up more of a fight but I was good with this scenario. If she refrained from being pissy with me, maybe I could talk her into dinner later tonight.

She had said no every day this week, but surely one of these days she'd succumb to me, right?

Outside, my Emily returned and she stepped away from my hand. Hey, no big, so long as she wasn't throwing daggers at me. I mean, yeah, I'd rather be touching her, but as long as she was going along with every other part of my plan, I could refrain from touching her for a little longer.

We passed Con's truck and I have to say, I was impressed to see she parallel parked that beast. It was an F-350 with a SuperCrew cab, so yeah, her parallel parking it? It was impressive.

So much so that maybe my dick was a bit impressed too.

But having a hard-on right now wouldn't do me any good, so I ignored it as I followed Em to my truck, parked a few spots down from where she parked Conor's truck.

Now, my truck wasn't nearly as big and impressive as Conor's but it was still a big truck. I only had a SuperCab, but I didn't have carseats and shit to pile in the cab so the half door to the backseats was more than enough for me.

I reached around her to pull the door open, which earned me one of Emily's signature glares. At this point in the game, I was thinking it was exactly that—a game. I was beginning to think she simply preferred to be cold and indifferent toward me, so she put on the farce in hopes to steer me away.

I wasn't going away.

Emily stepped up into my truck and when her ass hit leather, I closed the door on her, rounding the front to get in on the driver's side.

When I turned the ignition, I looked in her direction to see her staring straight ahead, her hands clasped in her lap, all while nibbling on the corner of her lip.

The movement plumped and pushed her lower lip, and I had to look away.

Goddamn, I didn't think the girl knew what she actually did to me.

"You have a make in mind?" I asked instead as I pulled away from the curb.

I glanced over at her while I repositioned my body, wrist on the steering wheel and leaning with my arm on top of the center console.

Her eyes glanced at my wrist before meeting mine. I fought against the desire to keep looking at her and turned my attention back to the road. It wasn't a busy road and it was pretty straight, but it wouldn't do me any good to injure her in an accident.

"No," she finally answered. "I figured just one of the larger dealerships would be fine. Just a car with good mileage."

"There's nothing you haven't seen and thought, 'Hmm, that's cute'." The last was said in a high falsetto and hearing her answering laugh made me grin wide.

"I guess maybe the new Fusions."

I grabbed my chest with the hand not steering the wheel. "A Ford girl. Be still my heart."

Again, Emily laughed and I had to shift in my seat. My jeans were growing uncomfortably tight.

Emily directing a laugh at me was something I didn't realize I was missing in life.

"It has nothing to do with Ford, and everything to do with the body style."

I had a joke on the tip of my tongue about body style but decided to keep it to myself, instead saying, "Alright. Well, to Mikkelson Ford we go."

CHAPTER TEN

EMILY

By mid-afternoon, I found myself in a white Ford Fusion with all the works. I didn't want all the works, would have been fine with cloth seats and a regular CD-radio unit, but Rory worked his male magic and I was the proud owner—co-owner—of a car with leather seats, satellite radio, and a rear camera.

At employee family pricing.

I felt pretty guilty about the last point, but Rory assured me that they were ripping me off by the tag price anyway.

Conor came out and helped with the paperwork, as Rory said he or Mia would, and when the three of us left, Rory pulled me aside and helped me into my car.

This wasn't the cocky Rory I knew. Self-assured Rory, yes, but not cocky. All day, whenever I tried to put the wall between us, he would go and do something or say something that made me smile and question what I thought about him.

Maybe he was changing.

I don't think he'd ever fought so hard for someone's attention before and it wasn't as if I were playing the cat-and-mouse game. But seeing him vie for something that wasn't coming to him as easily as everything else in his life did, was certainly shaping him into a different person.

"Dinner?" he asked me again, this time while I sat in my brand new car. He had his forearms on the top of the car and was leaning in toward me. I kept my eyes on his, searching for answers. I needed to know if this was a game.

If I was just a conquest to him.

I wasn't built like the girls he slept with. I thought I'd done really damn well over the last week, putting up the cinder block wall between the two of us, but I could feel it crumbling down.

I didn't want to be like the other girls.

When Rory was nice and kind, he was really nice and kind. I found myself liking him more and more when he left his cocky attitude at the door.

Still looking him in the eye, I sucked in my top lip and bit on it, concentrating. I watched as his pupils dilated and his nostrils flared, but still he said nothing.

"Ok."

It was barely spoken, hardly heard over the pounding of my heart, but Rory heard it loud and clear. His smile was movie-star worthy, showing that the man had a surprising dimple under his right eye, one that sat along his cheekbone. It added to the boyish quality he had.

"Awesome. Do you think you could be ready by seven?"

I nodded. "Sure. Is there going to be a dress code?"

"Just wear something nice. Not formal, just nice."

Because it was still warm in the evening, I chose a sleeveless sundress in white and turquoise. I did find a cardigan to pair with it if it started to get chilly. I debated on heels before finding a pair of slightly heeled sandals that wouldn't put my height over Rory's.

I had a thing against being taller than guys I was going out with.

Being tall my whole life, it was one of those things that I could either let bother me, or just go with. I let it bother me.

There was a knock on my apartment door just as I was applying lip gloss. I twisted the wand back in and headed toward the living area, grabbing my purse on the way. I pulled open the door and couldn't stop the smile from spreading when I saw Rory.

The man wore designer jeans to the bar, so it wasn't that he'd dressed up for me; he was wearing an outfit I'd seen him in before, even. It was that he paired it with a sport jacket and held a bouquet of daisies in his hand.

"You look great," he said, his eyes dropping and taking me in. "These are for you," he added, thrusting the flowers in my direction. It was slightly comical, the way he did it. I wasn't so sure that he was a flowers-to-girls guy generally.

"Thank you," I said, taking the bouquet from him. "Let me put these in a vase. You're welcome to come in." I moved to the kitchen, finding a vase above the fridge, and situated the white and baby pink blooms. I loved their simplicity.

Rory stood in the middle of my living room, his hands in his pockets which allowed his sport jacket to part in a way that had him looking all GQ-esque.

Not that he didn't any other day.

He still sported the stubble look and I was beginning to think it was just a new look for him, that he was going to keep it. It certainly didn't hurt his image. His hair was pulled back in the stubby ponytail again, but like I said, it didn't hurt his image.

"Ready?" I asked, stopping a little ways away from him. If I took a deep enough breath I could smell him from where I was. Any closer and I couldn't be held responsible for my actions.

"That's my line." His grin was crooked and he held a hand out to me, urging me closer to him. Without extra preamble, I took his hand in mine and allowed him to pull me close. I closed my eyes when I stood in front of him, allowing the moment to seep through my veins. When Rory pressed his lips to my temple, my lips lifted in a closed-lipped smile and I opened my eyes again, turning my head this time to look at him.

We were incredibly close. I could count the blue flecks in his left eye; there were five that made up the orb I previously thought was simply one blue piece in the sea of green. His eyes held mine captive and when the corners of his eyes crinkled, I could tell his grin was genuine.

"Let's eat."

Rory brought me to a nicer American Steakhouse near the coastline. We were seated on the patio, making me glad I grabbed my sweater. The breeze was gentle and the night was beginning to cool, but the atmosphere of the place was truly euphoric. They strung circle wicker lights throughout the patio and had patio heaters throughout.

After looking through the menu, I looked across the table and over the glass hurricane, toward Rory.

"You really do look beautiful tonight," he said, leaning onto his forearms. He linked his fingers together in front of him.

"Thank you."

"Thank you for finally agreeing to dinner." He chuckled lightly. "I'm enjoying spending time with you, Em."

Quietly, I admitted, "Me, too."

A week or two was awfully quick to change his ways, but maybe having a larger responsibility with O'Gallaghers did Rory some good. This entire week while pursing me, I hadn't noticed him checking out other women. I didn't see him persuading others to do things at his bidding.

I was about to tell him that I noticed the change in him when our waiter came.

"Thank you for joining us tonight. My name is Rick and I will be your server tonight. Have we decided on our entrees this evening?" he asked.

I nodded, as did Rory, who gestured toward me. "You go ahead."

Picking up the menu again to be sure, I found my item, reading it off for Rick. "I'll do the...ten ounce prime rib, please."

Rory's brows rose and I fought a giggle. I liked a good piece of red meat. I wasn't about to order a salad at a place like this.

After handing my menu to Rick, he turned his attention to Rory. "And for you, sir?"

Unlike me, Rory didn't need to open his menu. "I'll take your Maine Lobster Pot Pie."

I nearly bugged my eyes out of my head. I had seen that item on the menu; it was the one with the highest price tag.

And there Rory went, flaunting his money.

"Very well, sir. Any appetizers for the two of you?"

I shook my head but Rory answered, "An order of your caprese, please."

"All right." Rick took Rory's menu and folded them together in his hands. "We will have that appetizer out to you shortly."

"You've been here before, haven't you?" I asked, amused.

He nodded. "I have. When they opened, they brought some promotions to the pub and I checked it out."

"It's a very cute establishment," I said, glancing around the patio again.

The sun was a mere spot of orange over the water-filled horizon, and the beginning of a star-filled sky was starting to blanket above us. I watched as a plane's red lights flickered, flying in toward the mainland.

"The food is fantastic, too. I think you'll enjoy it."

His voice brought my eyes back to him. He held a hand out on top of the table and I allowed myself to place my hand in his. I couldn't stop the girly grin from starting as he lifted our hands to his lips, kissing my knuckles.

I had to remind myself that this was Rory's game.

But was it?

Was I different?

Or was I being a fool for allowing myself to be so drawn to Rory and his seductive ways?

I know I told myself one time with him, but I would not be opposed to bending that rule tonight. He was being incredibly kind and sweet, and it brought his sexy factor up to an eleven out of ten.

He lowered our hands back to the table, rubbing his thumb slowly over my knuckles now.

"Thank you again for finally agreeing to come out with me. I know we haven't had the best history, haven't started out on the right foot, but thank you for giving me this chance."

I internally battled with the need to tell him why I had kept my distance, but decided now wasn't the time or place. I wasn't sure that there ever would be a time or place, to be honest— unless he were to come out and simply ask.

Until then, I'd probably just keep my reasons to myself.

We were in the middle of discussing my school work and plans once the semester ended when Rick returned to the table. I let my fingers slip from Rory's as I returned both of my hands to my lap, allowing Rick to place the caprese between us.

"Here is your caprese. I also wanted to extend an apology," he was saying as he straightened. His attention was focused on Rory. "I was just informed we have run out of truffle. We can still make your meal, it would just be without that ingredient."

And that was when the Rory I had come to know, the one I'd heard about and hated, came out to play.

CHAPTER ELEVEN

RORY

God, she looked beautiful tonight.

Emily left her hair down. She curled it, sure, but it was down and I wanted nothing more than to run my fingers through the long locks.

The turquoise of her dress looked great against her skin, and it dipped just enough to show what minimal cleavage she had.

But it was still fucking beautiful.

She was fucking beautiful.

I didn't know how I got lucky enough for her to finally say yes, but I was certainly grateful.

There was also promise in her blue eyes that tonight might end my week-long celibacy streak. I couldn't wait to show her what I was truly capable of, to show her that last weekend was a fluke, a direct response to a year's worth of want and excitement.

Not that that made it sound any better.

Premature was premature, and was meant to be kept in the early teenaged years.

When Rick returned with our appetizer and Emily slipped her hand from mine, my body—my fucking soul—felt her leaving me.

"I also wanted to extend an apology," Rick was saying. I turned my attention from Emily to him. "I was just informed we have run out of truffle. We can still make your meal, it would just be without that ingredient."

I frowned, sitting up higher in my seat. "How do you run out of a key ingredient in your featured menu item?"

"I do apologize, sir."

"You'll be comping me for that cost then, I assume?" I didn't notice as Emily slouched further in her seat.

"I can certainly speak with the manager."

"How about you do that." The dry sarcasm in my voice was plenty evident, as was my displeasure in the situation.

How the hell did a restaurant run out of something that was a staple for their menu? Did they not have competent people running their ordering? You always planned for sales, and being short top ingredients was not the way to keep patrons walking in the doors.

Rick left and I shook my head. "Imbeciles," I muttered to myself in response to my last thought. I reached for my water glass, taking a sip before shaking my head again, grinning toward Emily. "Who runs out of ingredients?"

She sat up but her smile was nowhere to be found. She simply shrugged a shoulder, a frown on her face, as she looked down at the napkin in her lap. "It was an honest mistake, Rory. Maybe they didn't plan for a high ordering of one of their more expensive dishes."

"But you always plan. You always make sure you have enough and then some. Do we ever run out of items at O'Gallaghers? No," I answered for her. "We don't. And you know what? We stay in the black. They have these prices for a reason, Em. They can afford an extra few pounds of damned truffles."

"I don't know," she responded quietly, as if she had nothing else to say.

The caprese grew cold between us, as did the night. I wasn't sure exactly what was up with Emily. She went from happy and sexy, to her cold, withdrawn self. I reached for a piece of the appetizer to fill the gap of time. I tried to restart our earlier conversation about her schooling when she placed her napkin on the table.

"I'd like to go home now." Her voice was quiet and her body language was completely closed down.

I frowned. "We haven't even gotten our entrees yet."

"Rory, what you just did was embarrassing." Emily's voice was still quiet and she leaned into the table as if she were attempting to keep her voice from traveling. Her eyes were widened yet weary. "You could have been more effective by simply saying 'ok,' rather than make that man feel like a heel for something that wasn't even his fault."

"But—"

"No," she cut me off, holding a hand up. "I'd like to go home now."

I stared at her, fucking baffled. What in the ever loving hell just happened?

She stood, opening her purse while doing so, and dropped a couple twenties on the table.

"Jesus, Em, I'll cover the damn bill," I said, my irritation starting to come to surface. I stood, pulling my wallet from my back pocket, and replaced her bills with my own, holding hers out in front of me. She reluctantly took them and started for the restaurant, leaving me behind.

I shrugged into my sport jacket and followed, still confused as all get out as to what just happened. So she was embarrassed? Didn't mean she couldn't enjoy her dinner. We could laugh about it later. Why did we have to go without enjoying ourselves a little more?

I reached her in the middle of the inside dining area, but when I moved to place a hand on her back—possessively, yes; fuckers were looking at her—she stepped away from me.

I could feel those same fuckers laughing behind my back.

She wanted to play this way? She wanted to go back to bitch mode? Well so fucking-be-it.

We waited in silence by valet as my truck was retrieved. Valet helped her into the cab, so I just walked around to get in myself. After being sure she was situated, by quick glance only, I threw the truck in drive and headed back to her place.

The entire drive was made in silence. It allowed me to stew on her words and her reactions.

She fucking stepped away from me, putting more distance between us when I had been pretty sure that wall was fucking eradicated.

She was unbuckled before I could even turn the truck off at her place, out her door before I could get my own belt to unlock. "Goddammit, Emily," I said, frustrated, as I moved after her.

"You don't have to walk me to my door." She was looking through her purse as she walked. She pulled out her keys as she reached the stairwell, jogging up them in a pretty impressive fashion, seeing as she was in heeled shoes.

"I'm walking you to your damn door," I muttered, only a few steps behind.

Emily unlocked her door in probably the quickest time I'd ever seen a key insert and twist, and she was sliding through the doorway. I pushed in after her before she could slam the door on my face.

"I don't want to talk to you right now." Her voice was still devoid of emotion, very much the Emily I had known for the last year.

"What the hell is your problem?" I let my irritation come through, but I didn't fucking care.

She whipped back toward me, her hair flying. "You are, Rory! You!"

"Me? What the fuck did I do?" My voice was raised as loud as hers.

"You're such a goddamned child, Rory. You don't behave like that in public. You are a grown man. Not only that, but you run a respected establishment. Just like that restaurant. How would you like it if someone acted the way you did?"

"We don't run out of shit." I stood in my spot, arms crossed over my chest.

"Oh, so O'Gallaghers is better than everyone else. Just like you fucking think you are."

I lifted my brows, but kept my arms crossed. "Oh-ho, tell me how you really feel, Emily."

She threw her purse down on the couch and came up to me, toe to toe, eye to eye. Her slight chest brushed my forearms and I watched as her mouth tightened in anger, her chest heaving with pent up anger and emotion.

Well guess what, Cupcake? You and me both.

"You are a cocky asshole who thinks he's better than everyone! You are the least genuine person I have ever had the misfortune of knowing. You are all about the bottom line and don't care how you get what you want. You're self-centered, materialistic, and heaven forbid you take on a client for your," she waved her hand in the air, "other business—who actually needs your fucking help. But no, because they don't fit in with your ideals and who you think is worthy of your time, you push them aside to figure things out on their own."

"At least people know what they're getting with me. I don't lead people on. The women all know what I'm about, and my clientele and team thank me for what I bring to the table, because I'm helping further their careers. You, on the other hand, are a fucking block of ice. Who the hell knows what they're gonna get with you? Sweet in the middle? I thought so, but apparently that was all a fucking façade too. Embarrassing is leaving a restaurant before they've even given you your meal."

She just shook her head minutely, not saying a word as her eyes stayed locked with mine.

Finally, she spoke up, her voice strong, but quieter than before. "You need to grow up and become an adult, Rory." She stepped away. "I'll be sure Conor knows to not put us on the schedule together, ever. I don't want to deal with you anymore."

She turned away and part of me wanted to follow her, to finish this fucking fight, but the other part was as done with her as she was with me.

Good fucking riddance.

CHAPTER TWELVE

That night was fucking hell.

I tried scrolling through my phone for a quick hook-up, but every time my thumb hovered over the connect button, it was Emily's face I saw.

No, not the yelling one I recently encountered, but her shining blue eyes, her wide smile as she laughed, and her fucking gorgeous blonde hair.

I really hated conceding to people's opinions, but I spent the entire night—no joke, the entire fucking night—replaying her words.

Was I really that shallow?

Like I said, the women I slept with knew the score going in.

And I really didn't see anything wrong with choosing clients who were well on their way in their fitness journeys. It made sense. You give them a product, they have a quick turn-around time, they post the hell out of that shit on social media, and you had more orders.

But maybe I should look into taking on a client or two who actually, truly, needed the service. It would take longer to get to the end goal, but maybe that wasn't such a bad thing.

I went through every fucking email, deleted ones too, trying to find people I could add to my client base. It was three in the damn morning, but I still responded to their emails.

I ended up finding five additional people to add to my

clientele. What was adding five more going to do for my time? Not a whole lot. It wasn't going to eat much more than my current base was.

At four, I emailed the owner of the Steakhouse, apologizing and offering a hefty tab at O'Gallaghers if he ever wanted to stop by.

I suppose part of this was easy because I wasn't doing it face to face, but there was one face to face I was going to have to do.

That I wanted to do.

Putting aside my laptop for the night, I closed my eyes and took a nap.

She was opening tomorrow. I'd find her then.

CHAPTER THIRTEEN

EMILY

I arrived to O'Gallaghers early the next day, thankful to see Stone was opening with me. He didn't do many early shifts so I didn't get to work with him often, but he was a fun guy. He made everything light and easy.

Things I was definitely needing today.

I was under a bit of an emotional hangover today after letting out every single thing I'd been holding back with Rory. I should have known the good was going to fade, that he couldn't be as great as he was showing me over the week.

I entered O'Gallaghers through the back, not thinking about the fact I'd be passing Rory's staircase, but thankful just the same when I didn't see him. The kitchen was quiet but music was playing in the bar area. Stone was probably setting up his coolers 'just the right way.' It was funny to me how such a big guy could be so OCD about something as trivial as lemon and lime placement.

"Hey, Stone," I started, as I pushed through the doors, but my words were cut off by the man sitting at the bar, facing the doors as if he were waiting for me.

"Emily."

I clenched my jaw and lifted my chin. "Rory." I moved down the bar toward Stone, who was indeed working out his coolers. "What can I do to help?"

"If you want to get towels together, that would be great."

Ignoring Rory, I moved to the back to do as Stone asked, grabbing enough for the first hours before they were due to be changed out. As I was about to push through the door again, it opened back toward me and Rory stepped in.

I was expecting a pissed off look on his face; instead, there was a thoughtful one.

"I'd like to talk to you." Before I could answer, he added, "Stone is aware and is ok if you take a few minutes."

This was a really difficult place to be. On the one hand, I wanted so badly to tell him off again. I didn't want to—couldn't—deal with the emotional backlash again. But on the other, he was my boss and I did need this job for at least the next few months. There was only so much Conor could do; he wasn't the only one running O'Gallaghers.

I set the towels and bucket of sanitizer water down and headed toward the office, the only place we could shut the door and have privacy. I refused to think of other things we did in this very space.

"About last night." He took a deep, audible breath. "I did some thinking."

I crossed my arms. He could think all he damn wanted. He could keep thinking for all I cared.

"I want to change."

I stuck my tongue in between my teeth, biting down gently. I wasn't entirely sure how to respond so I didn't. I wasn't expecting him to say that.

"You helped me come to the realization that I have room to grow as a person. You and Con, really. He said something earlier in the week that rang along the same lines as what you said." Rory stuffed a hand in his jeans pocket and ran the other through his hair, holding it against the back of his head as he kept his focus on me.

"I really enjoyed the time we had together. When I wasn't being a dick, that is. I'd like to work on being a better person, a person who you believe in. I never had a hard time looking in the mirror until after you told me what you saw negatively in me. It really had me thinking."

I shook my head and sighed. "Rory, no. We can't..." I shook my head again. I felt myself completely thaw toward him. There wasn't anything worse in the world than feeling like you had to change for someone and I hated that I did that to him.

I was glad he wanted to make the changes, but I didn't want him to make them for me. We didn't have a future. The moments we had, short as they were, had some fun mixed in, but I was leaving in a few months. "It would probably just be better for everyone if we just ended this here and now. I'm done in four months. I don't know where I'll go after graduation, if I'll be staying in San Diego or if I decide to go elsewhere for school. Heck, it depends on where I get into the anesthesia program. You're my boss and it's just better, healthier, for everyone involved if we just kept it that way."

I wasn't sure what his reaction would be, but the thoughtful look on his face wasn't what I would have bet on.

"Ok."

I couldn't help it; I frowned. "Just like that?"

His smile wasn't coy, it wasn't cocky. It wasn't full and assured, either. It was actually kind of sad. "I'm going to prove to you that I can change. I'll give you your space but I'm not going to let this go."

I couldn't stop my grin this time. There he went again, all sure of himself.

"Rory, no." I uncrossed my arms and stuck my fingers in my back pockets. "Do you, Rory. When you're not being an ass, you have a certain energy about you. Don't change that for me. Don't change that for anyone. You have the ability to be a great guy, but I just don't think you and I could be healthy together. Too much negativity between us."

Rory stepped close to me but I held my ground. I wasn't

sure what his next move would be.

I was honest with my words.

When Rory was being a good guy, he truly was an awesome man to get to know. If he stuck with that, he'd make one lucky woman very happy.

He'd have to figure out the monogamy thing, sure, but I thought he was on his way to being an adult.

"Whatever you want to think, Em. But I'm going to prove you wrong." With that, he put his hands on my shoulders and leaned in to kiss my forehead.

Before I could react, he was gone.

EPILOGUE

EMILY

I graduated my nursing program with honors.

Surprising, yes.

But with the help of a changed schedule, and the ability to get places faster, I was able to put more energy into studying and passed my remaining tests with flying colors. One of the prerequisites for the nurse anesthesia program was a minimum of one year in a critical care setting, so I chose to apply to a number of ICUs in the Bay Area, eventually accepting a position in a pediatric ICU. It was extremely difficult to work with critically ill children, but it also was incredibly rewarding.

When it was time to apply to my next school, I was quickly accepted to a Nursing Anesthesia program in Arizona, thanks to my previous grades and letters of recommendation from peers. With my new income, I was able to get my auto loan out of Conor's name and fully into mine too. Conor joked that he was sad to be cutting yet another tie with me, but I assured both him and Mia that I would come back around. The O'Gallaghers had become a pseudo-extended family of sorts, and I enjoyed spending time with them.

Rory too.

Over the last eighteen months, not once did he approach me

about furthering this...thing...we had between us, and if he was continuing with his sexual endeavors the way he had before our little office party, he'd become incredibly secretive of it.

He was in the pub more often, doing more of the day-to-day tasks while Conor took over much of the bookkeeping. With two babies at home under three, Conor and Mia had their hands full.

Rumor had it Rory was also doing more one-on-one coaching with his clientele.

I suppose it wasn't so much of a rumor, as I saw him spending time at the beach helping a heavier woman with exercises she could easily do without equipment or a gym.

I was prud of who he was becoming.

But that was now all in my past.

O'Gallaghers, and its people, was now a piece of my history and I was moving on to the next phase of my life.

Nursing anesthesia school was no joke, and I was fully prepared to study my ass off. Between work and studying, I would have little time for a social life, but that was something I was used to.

I was coming home from my first day of classes, folders and papers and syllabi in hand, completely prepared to get a head start on studying. It would be another year or so until I received my clinical experience, but I wanted to be absolutely sure I knew the science behind everything I was going to learn.

I parked my car in the driveway of the house I was renting and was a little concerned that there was a car parked along the street that I didn't recognize.

But then again, I was new to town and didn't recognize many of the cars in the neighborhood yet.

After parking my car in the garage, I stepped out, shouldering my backpack, and was rounding the end of the car to head inside when a tall shadow fell into my garage.

With a startled yelp, I put my hand to my chest and turned, hoping to God it was just a friendly neighbor and not some psycho out to get the new neighbor.

I maybe watched a scary movie last night.

In my dark house.

With minimal furniture.

I don't know what I'd been thinking, either.

"You startled me," I said to the faceless stranger, only to gasp aloud when the person moved from the shadows, showing his face.

RORY

I spent a lot of time giving Emily her space.

And in that time—eighteen months, to be exact—my hand and arm got a little sore because that was the only action my cock was getting.

I was hell bent on proving to her that I could be a good guy, a guy she could believe in, and hell, a fucking grown up.

I certainly proved it to Conor, who gave me more responsibilities at the bar because he trusted I would run the bar as he would. And because of that, I felt like shit when I gave him the news.

I had one last person to prove myself to, and I hoped to fucking God she would be as understanding, as open, as Con had been.

Emily left O'Gallaghers a year ago. She stopped in on occasion, but she no longer worked for us. And then she moved.

She fucking moved, and I felt that shit.

I knew that I was hung up on her, knew it the week I begged her to dinner. But her moving did things to me.

Sure, it was only a few states and only a five hour drive, but I wanted her close.

Shit, that made me sound like the insensitive ass she accused me of being earlier last year.

I wanted her close and I was willing to make those changes to have it happen.

Better?

Thought so.

I moved out of the apartment above the pub and it actually stood vacant right now. Brenna stated her living arrangements worked for her and Con and I didn't exactly want a stranger living up there.

So I vacated the apartment.

I gave Con my news.

And I hopped on a plane.

Arizona was warm in the early spring, not much different than San Diego, but I didn't find myself sweating over the heat as I stood outside the house my GPS brought me to.

No, I was sweating over fucking nerves.

How would she react? What would she say? Should I maybe have called instead?

Probably.

Fuck.

She'd go and probably say how self-assured I was, when really this was the most fucking vulnerable I'd been in years.

When the little white Fusion came pulling into the garage, I walked around, wanting to see her. I didn't intend to scare the girl and when she gasped, I took a step back and held up my hands. "It's just me, Em."

She dropped her chin and frowned. "Rory?"

Her hair was pulled up on top of her head so I couldn't get my fill of that. Instead, I was able to appreciate just about every other facet of her. She wore white shorts and a flannel, and was sexy as hell in the ensemble.

Arizona looked good on her.

"Hey, Emily."

Hey, Emily?

You mean to tell me, after all the thinking on the plane and the drive over here, all I could come up with was Hey, Emily?

She dropped her backpack to the ground beside her and, still frowning, made her way toward me. "What are you doing here? Why aren't you back home?"

"I don't currently have a home." Hey, it was the truth. Go big or go... Well, you know.

If anything though, her frown deepened. I reached out and smoothed my thumb over the ridges. "That'll get stuck, Em."

She shook her head, which had me pulling my thumb away, but she didn't look pissed. No, she looked confused. "Why are you in Arizona? Why aren't you back in San Diego?"

I took a deep breath and launched in with the words I wanted to say. "I have tried really hard over the last year, year and half, to be the type of man you could count on. You don't need a man, hell, you'll probably tell me you don't have time for a man, but I want to be there for you. I want to show you I've changed. I want to hold your hand. I want to make you dinner on those nights you're scrambling to figure out how you're going to juggle food and work and studying and walking the dog."

"I don't have a dog."

I grinned and held up my finger. "We can take this at your pace, Em, but this is something I want to do. A journey I want to take. Please give me that opportunity."

She was quiet, staring at me. I had the gut sinking feeling she was going to say no.

Conor would take me back. Hell, he'd probably welcome me back with open arms. Brenna had taken some of my responsibilities, but I wasn't sure how that would pan out in the end. I also had a place to live above the bar.

But what was life without the person you had a feeling you were meant to spend it with?

When she still didn't answer, I took a deep breath, letting it out slowly. With a sad grin, I reached for her hand, needing some sort of contact with her one last time before I walked away. I squeezed once and stepped back.

"Ok. Alright."

I took another step back and when she still didn't move, I turned.

I was going to leave with my pride. I wasn't going to beg.

The desert looked a little drier, was a little warmer, and was definitely browner, as I made my way back to the rental car.

EMILY

This was all so surreal.

Rory was here.

Rory was here, in Arizona, at the house I was renting.

And he was walking away.

He was walking away and was going to head back to San Diego.

Did I trust that he could have changed? Well, yes, actually. I witnessed the small changes. Did I think he could keep those small changes?

Would I hate myself if I didn't at least give it a shot?

Hell, I really didn't have time for a relationship! But who was to say he'd still be around in three years when I graduated? The fact that he apparently waited a year and half was damn impressive.

I heard a car start and I shook my head, forcing myself back to the here and now.

He was leaving and it made me come to a realization.

I couldn't let him leave.

I bolted out of my garage and ran down the slight drive, jumping in front of what had been the mysterious car, all while praying he wouldn't gun it, leaving this place in his haste.

I stared at him through the windshield.

He stared back.

And when I smiled at him, he smiled back.

And he knew, just as I did, that I was giving him his chance.

We would figure it out. And if it didn't work, it didn't work.

But we could at least say we tried.

Because when his cocky side was gone, and my cold indifference melted, I really enjoyed being around him.

This wasn't going to be easy.

We had hardly been anything other than friends over the past year and half, and we were jumping into something more.

...but it was going to be worth the ride.

Did you enjoy Rory and Emily's happy for now novella?
Please consider leaving a review on Amazon!
Also, be sure to check out the Troublemakers: Mignon Mykel's
reader group on Facebook!

Continue reading for a look at All Night Long: Brenna's story.

If you're looking to read Rory and Emily's HEA,
consider picking up Hot Holiday Nights, available in the
O'Gallagher Nights boxset, as well as digitally, on its own!

ALL NIGHT LONG PREVIEW

For as long as I could remember, I've lived under the protective shadow of my older brothers. We were all fairly spread apart in age, at least in comparison to my friends who were one year, maybe two years, three years at most apart from the other kids in their families.

But for my brothers and me? We had the four year gap.

Well, technically Rory and Conor were three years apart but their birthdates were on opposite ends of the year.

So pretty much four years.

That meant I never went to the same school as Conor, who is eight years older than me.

It also meant that there had only been two years in elementary school, no years in middle school, and one four-quarter period in in the space of life that was known as high school, that I had with Rory.

That did not stop the two of them from threatening every kid they ran across though.

People knew who I was.

If there were such a thing in our little beach town, I would have been considered royalty with the way my brothers watched over me.

By ten—ten!—I decided I needed to find a way to step away from the pampered role everyone saw me in, so I set out to do just that.

Away from my brothers' eyes, of course.

Which only made their unwavering faith in me feel like a dagger through the heart, with every omission of truth I told them.

Or the little parts of my life that I didn't tell them. The little parts that made the large sum of who I was.

The things that they considered rumors.

I pushed away good friends so I could fit in.

I'm ashamed to say I spread my legs to ruin that 'good girl' reputation my brothers molded for me.

By day, I was Sweet Brenna O'Gallagher, the girl who could do no wrong in her brothers' eyes.

But everyone else knew who I really was.

They knew the slutty girl, the one who wore low cut tops and too much eye makeup.

The girl who was known behind hands as the one who fucked a senior in his van her freshman year.

Then rumors spread about other things.

STDs. Drugs. Pregnancies.

While most of those rumors I could give a big 'fuck you' to, there was one rumor that hit incredibly close to home, one that wasn't a rumor at all.

And every time I heard it, every time I saw someone whispering behind their hands, their eyes avoiding mine but looking for tell-tale signs, the pain in my gut, in my heart, was so incredibly agonizing that I could not bear to be that person anymore.

So I vowed off men the year I turned nineteen.

Nineteen.

The time most girls were starting to find who they were.

I had already found who I was and I didn't like her. I didn't like what she did to her body, what she did to her head, what she did to her heart.

I was successful at keeping men at bay for two years.

Granted, the rumors turned into 'cock tease' but that was infinitely better than what they had been.

Two years my vow of celibacy, of staying away from men, wasn't even tempted to change. But then my brothers hired him.

Greyson Stone.

Stone to everyone. Grey to just me.

Behind closed doors.

Behind our hands. Away from public. Away from my brothers.

Just like every other aspect of who I truly was, I was extremely good at hiding this relationship from my brothers.

But Grey was threatening to change that.

Five years, he let me have him in secret.

Five years, and he knew who I really was, who I hid from my brothers. He knew and he wanted to expose me.

Expose us.

So what could I do but try and push him away?

AVAILABLE NOW!

ACKNOWLEDGEMENTS

The O'Gallaghers have been a fun trio of siblings to write about. Thank you for welcoming them into your world. Every time a book is purchased or is read, I have a moment of pause. The fact that people read words I have written is still completely mind-boggling to me.

And I hope that it always will be.

Thank you to Jenn, my editor. I know you enjoyed Rory in One Night Stand, and I can only hope he lived up to some of your expectations. Thank you for dealing with my schedule changes and last minute planning. Nothing like giving you one manuscript, quickly followed by another with a note: Do this one first! You rock, lady.

To my family and friends who don't ask when I'm going to return home. I honestly believe that this move I made is partially responsible for me being able to accomplish my dreams. Thank you for your support in everything I've been doing.

ABOUT MIGNON MYKEL

Mignon Mykel is the author of the Love In All Places series. When not sitting at Starbucks writing whatever her characters tell her to, you can find her hiking in the mountains of Arizona. Mignon writes in one world, so while every series can be read as a standalone, her stories will be more enjoyable if you read them in publication order.

LOVE IN ALL PLACES *series*
full series reading order

Interference **(Prescott Family)**
O'Gallagher Nights: The Complete Series
Troublemaker **(Prescott Family)***
Saving Grace **(Loving Meadows)**
Breakaway **(Prescott Family)***
Altercation **(Prescott Family)***
27: Dropping the Gloves **(Enforcers of San Diego)**
32: Refuse to Lose **(Enforcers of San Diego)**
Holding **(Prescott Family)***
A Holiday for the Books **(Prescott Family)**
25: Angels and Assists **(Enforcers of San Diego)**
From the Beginning **(Prescott Family)**

* *The Playmaker Duet (Troublemaker, Breakaway, Altercation, Holding)*
can be enjoyed in one easy boxed set.

Printed in Great Britain
by Amazon